THE TALE OF JOLLY ROBIN

ARTHUR SCOTT BAILEY

THE TALE OF JOLLY ROBIN

I

NESTLINGS

Of course, there was a time, once, when Jolly Robin was just a nestling himself. With two brothers and one sister—all of them, like him, much spotted with black—he lived in a house in one of Farmer Green's apple trees.

The house was made of grass and leaves, plastered on the inside with mud, and lined with softer, finer grass, which his mother had chosen with the greatest care.

But Jolly never paid much attention to his first home. What interested him more than anything else was food. From dawn till dark, he was alwayscheeping for something to eat. And since the other children were just as hungry as he was, those four growing babies kept their parents busy finding food for them. It was then that Jolly Robin learned to like angleworms. And though he ate greedily of insects and bugs, as well as wild berries, he liked angleworms best.

Jolly and his sister and his brothers could always tell when their father or their mother brought home some dainty, because the moment the parent lighted upon the limb where the nest was built they could feel their home sink slightly, from the added weight upon the branch.

Then the youngsters would set up a loud squalling, with a great craning of necks and stretching of orange-colored mouths.

Sometimes, when the dainty was specially big, Mr. or Mrs. Robin would say, "Cuck! cuck!" That meant "Open wide!" But they seldom found it necessary to give that order.

Somehow, Jolly Robin managed to eat more than the rest of the nestlings. And so he grew faster than the others. He soon learned a few tricks, too. For instance, if Mrs. Robin happened to be sitting on the nest, to keep her family warm, when Mr. Robin returned with a lunch for the children, Jolly had a trick that he played on his mother, in case she didn't move off the nest fast enough to suit him.

He would whisper to the rest of the children. And then they would jostle their fond parent, lifting her up above them, and sometimes almost upsetting her, so that she had hard work to keep from falling off the nest.

Mrs. Robin did not like that trick very well. But she knew that Jolly would not annoy her with it long. Indeed, he was only eleven days old when he left his birthplace and went out into the wide world.

You see, the young folk grew so fast that they soon more than filled the house. So there was nothing their parents could do but persuade them to leave home and learn to fly.

One day, therefore, Mr. Robin did not bring his children's food to the edge of the nest and drop it into their mouths. Instead, he stood on the limb a little distance away from them and showed them a plump angleworm.

The sight of that dainty was more than Jolly Robin could resist. He scrambled boldly out of the nest; and tottering up to his father on his wobbling legs, he snatched the tempting morsel out of his proud parent's bill.

Jolly never went back to the nest after that. The next day Mrs. Robin coaxed the other children from home in the same fashion. And though it may seem a heartless act, it was really the best thing that could have happened to Jolly and his sister and his brothers.

You see, they had to learn to fly. And so long as they stayed in the nest they could never learn a difficult feat like flying.

II
LEARNING TO FLY

After Jolly Robin had gulped down the fat angleworm with which his father had coaxed him to leave the nest, he clung desperately to the limb. With no food in sight he had plenty of time to look about him and to be alarmed.

The day was not gone before he had a great fright. He tumbled out of the apple tree and fell squawking and fluttering upon the ground.

Luckily, his mother happened to be at home. She went to Jolly at once and told him not to be afraid.

"Nothing will hurt you," she said, "if you'll only keep still. But if you squall like that, the cat will find you."

It may seem strange, but his mother's words frightened Jolly all the more. They scared him so thoroughly that he stopped making a noise, anyhow. And that was how he learned never to talk when he was on the ground near a house where a cat might live.

"Now," said Jolly's mother, as soon as he was still, "I'll teach you a new game. Just watch me!" And spreading her wings, she flapped them, and sprang into the air.

Soon Jolly was trying to imitate her. And it was not long before he found himself gliding a short distance, skimming along just off the ground.

But in spite of all his efforts, he couldn't help falling again. Though his mother tried to show him how to fly into a tree-top, Jolly Robin seemed unable to learn the trick.

At last Mr. Robin said to his wife:

"I'll teach him the rest. You've made a good beginning. But he must learn more at once. There's no telling when the cat may come into the orchard to hunt for field-mice. And you know what would happen then."

His wife shuddered. But Mr. Robin told her not to worry.

"I'll soon have this youngster so he can fly as well as anybody," he declared.

So he went and hopped about on the ground with Jolly for a little while, showing him how to find worms beneath the grass carpet of the orchard.

And then, in a loud voice, Mr. Robin suddenly cried:

"The cat! The cat!" And he flew into an old tree near-by.

Jolly Robin had never seen Farmer Green's cat. But he had heard that she was a dreadful, fierce creature. And when his father shouted her name Jolly was so startled that he forgot he didn't quite know how to fly. Before he knew what he was doing, he followed his father right up into the old apple tree and perched himself on a low branch.

That was the way he learned to fly, for he never had the least trouble about it afterward. And as soon as he realized that he had actually flown from the ground to the bough he was so pleased that he began to laugh merrily.

As for the cat, she was not in the orchard at all. Indeed, Jolly's father had not said that she was. You see, he had played a joke on his son.

Now, up to that time Jolly Robin had not been named. You must remember that he was not two weeks old. And having three other children of the same age, his parents had not been able to think of names for all of them.

But this big youngster laughed so heartily that his father named him "Jolly," on the spot. And "Jolly" he remained ever afterward.

III

THE WIDE, WIDE WORLD

After he learned to fly, Jolly Robin's father took him into the woods to spend each night in a roost where there were many other young robins, whose fathers had likewise brought them there.

Jolly learned a great deal from being with so many new friends. It was not long before he could find plenty of food for himself, without help from anyone.

He discovered, too, that there was safety in numbers. For example, if Jasper Jay made too great a nuisance of himself by bullying a young robin, a mob of robins could easily put Jasper to flight.

"Always help other people!" That was a motto that all the youngsters had to learn. And another was this: "Follow your father's lead!"

Later in the season, in October, when the robin cousins and uncles and aunts and sisters and brothers and all the rest of the relations made their long journey to their winter homes in the South, Jolly found that there was a good reason for such rules. If he hadn't followed his father then he might have lost his way, because—since it was the first time he had ever been out of Pleasant Valley—he knew nothing whatever about travelling.

He looked forward with much interest to the journey, for as the days grew shorter he heard a great deal of talk about the trip among his elders. And while he was waiting for the day when they should leave he became acquainted with many new and delicious morsels to eat. He roamed about picking wild grapes, mulberries and elderberries. And he did not scorn a large, green katydid when he chanced to find one.

There was always some new dainty to be sampled; though as the weather grew colder Jolly began to understand that in winter Pleasant Valley would not be so fine a place to live.

However, he managed to find food enough so that he continued to grow rapidly. The night after he found a mountain ash on a hillside, full of bright red berries, his father said that he seemed much taller than he had been that morning.

"You must have eaten a great many of those berries," said Mr. Robin.

"Well, I notice one thing," Jolly observed. "My waistcoat is fast losing its black spots. And it's redder than it was. The red berries certainly colored it in some way."

Mr. Robin replied that he had never heard of such a thing happening. He looked curiously at his son's waistcoat.

"It does seem to look different," he said. "It's brighter than it was."

Really, that was only because Jolly was fast growing up. But neither he nor his father stopped to think of that. And since Jolly had learned that motto, "Follow your father's lead," he thought his waistcoat ought to be just as red as old Mr. Robin's was.

So Jolly visited the mountain ash each day and fairly stuffed himself with the bright red fruit.

It did him no harm, anyhow. And he enjoyed eating it.

And the next spring, when Jolly Robin returned to Pleasant Valley, after spending the winter in the South, there was not a redder waistcoat than his in all the neighborhood.

IV

WHAT JOLLY DID BEST

Jolly Robin had something on his mind. For several days he had been turning a certain matter over in his head. But in spite of all his thinking, he seemed unable to find any answer to the question that was troubling him. So at last he decided he would have to ask somebody to help him.

And that was why Jolly stopped Jimmy Rabbit near the garden one day.

"I want your advice," he told Jimmy Rabbit.

"Certainly!" that young gentleman replied. And he sat himself down upon his wheelbarrow and looked very earnest. "If it's anything about gardening," he said, "I should advise you to raise cabbages, by all means."

But Jolly Robin said he wasn't thinking of planting a garden.

"In fact," he explained, "the trouble is, I don't know what to do. I'd like to have some regular work, you know. And since you've had a good deal of experience, having run a tooth-pulling parlor, a barber-shop, and a shoe-store, I thought you might be able to tell me what would be a good business for me to take up."

For a few minutes Jimmy Rabbit did not speak. But he nodded his head wisely.

"Let me see!" he said at last. "What's the thing you do best?"

Jolly Robin replied at once that he thought he could fly better than he could do anything else. And he felt so happy, because he was sure Jimmy Rabbit was going to help him, that he began to laugh gaily. And he couldn't help singing a snatch of a new song he had heard that morning. And then he laughed again.

"You're mistaken," Jimmy Rabbit said to him. "You fly well enough, I dare say. But there are others who can beat you at flying.... No!" he declared. "What you can do better than anybody I know is to laugh. And if I were you I should make laughing my regular business."

8

That idea struck Jolly Robin as being so funny that he laughed harder than ever. And Jimmy Rabbit nodded his head again, as if to say, "I'm right and I know it!"

At last Jolly Robin stopped laughing long enough to ask Jimmy to explain how anyone could make a business of laughing. "I don't see how it could be done," said Jolly Robin.

"Why—it's simple enough!" Jimmy told him. "All you need do is to find somebody who will hire you to laugh for him. There are people, you know, who find it very difficult to laugh. I should think they'd be glad to pay somebody to do their laughing for them."

"Name someone!" Jolly Robin urged him.

And Jimmy Rabbit did.

"There's old Mr. Crow!" he said. "You know how solemn he is. It's positively painful to hear him try to laugh at a joke. I'm sure he would be delighted with this idea. And if I were you I'd see him before somebody else does."

Jolly Robin looked puzzled.

"Who would ever think of such a thing but you?" he asked.

"Nobody!" Jimmy Rabbit replied. "But I like the scheme so well that I almost wish I hadn't mentioned it. And unless you make your bargain with old Mr. Crow at once I may decide to go into the laughing business myself.... My advice to you," he said, "is to hurry!"

So Jolly Robin thanked him. And then he flew away to find old Mr. Crow.

Of course, he went to the cornfield first.

V

LAUGHING FOR MR. CROW

Sure enough! old Mr. Crow was in the cornfield. And though he was feeling somewhat peevish that morning, because a coon had disturbed his rest the night before, he listened to what Jolly Robin had to say.

"I've come to ask you a question," Jolly told him. "I've decided to go into business—the laughing business. And I want to inquire if you wouldn't like to engage me to do your laughing for you."

Well, that struck old Mr. Crow as being very funny. He forgot all about his loss of sleep. And his eye twinkled quite merrily. He tried to laugh, too; but it was a pitiful attempt—no more than a hoarse cackle, which was, as Jimmy Rabbit had said, positively painful. Old Mr. Crow seemed to realize that he was making a very queer sound. He hastily turned his laugh into a cough and pretended that he had a kernel of corn stuck in his throat.

"What are your prices?" he asked Jolly Robin. "Are you going to charge by the day or by the laugh?"

"Just as you prefer!" Jolly answered.

"Well, I'll have to think about it," old Mr. Crow told him. "It's a question that I wouldn't care to decide in a hurry. If I paid you by the day you might not laugh at all. And if I paid you by the laugh you might laugh all the time.... It would be pretty expensive, either way. And I don't believe I'd like that."

"I'll tell you what I'll do," said Jolly Robin then. "I'll stay with you one day for nothing. And we'll see how the arrangement suits us."

That suggestion pleased Mr. Crow.

"Agreed!" he said quickly. "And now," he added, "you may laugh for me, because I am quite delighted."

So Jolly Robin laughed happily. And old Mr. Crow remarked that it was a fair laugh, though not so loud as he would have liked.

"I'll do better next time," Jolly assured him.

"Good!" said Mr. Crow. "And now, since I've finished my breakfast, we'll go over to the woods and see what's going on there this morning."

The first person they saw in the woods was Peter Mink. He was fishing for trout in Broad Brook. And old Mr. Crow, as soon as he spied him, sang out:

"How many of Farmer Green's fish have you eaten this morning?"

Peter Mink was just crawling out of the water, with a fish in his mouth. When he heard Mr. Crow calling to him, he dropped his trout upon a rock and looked up quickly.

"How much of Farmer Green's corn have you stolen for your breakfast?" he cried.

At that Jolly Robin began to laugh. But Mr. Crow stopped him quickly.

"Don't laugh!" the old gentleman squawked. "There's nothing to laugh at, so far as I can see."

So Jolly managed to smother his laughter, for he noticed that Mr. Crow was angry.

"You'll have to be careful," Mr. Crow warned him. "You mustn't laugh at the wrong time, you know."

"I'll do my best," Jolly Robin promised. And he could see already that old Mr. Crow was going to be hard to please.

VI

TICKLING A NOSE

Old Mr. Crow did not want to stay near the brook to talk with Peter Mink. Calling to Jolly Robin to follow him, he flapped his way to the edge of the woods and sat in a tree overlooking the pasture.

"Here comes Tommy Fox!" Mr. Crow exclaimed. "We ought to have some fun with him. So when it's time for you to laugh for me, don't forget to laugh loudly."

"I'll remember," Jolly promised him. And just by way of practice he chirruped so merrily that Tommy Fox pricked up his ears and came bounding up to the tree where Jolly and Mr. Crow were sitting.

"Good morning!" Mr. Crow cried to Tommy. "Is that a hen's feather that's stuck behind your ear?" he asked very solemnly.

"No!" said Tommy Fox. "It's a crow's; and I certainly had a fine breakfast."

Now, Jolly Robin wasn't quite sure whether he ought to laugh or not. And then Tommy winked at him. So Jolly thought there must be a joke somewhere and he began to chirrup as loudly as he could.

"For pity's sake, keep still!" old Mr. Crow snapped.

"But you wanted me to laugh louder," Jolly reminded him.

"Yes," said Mr. Crow — "when there's anything to laugh at."

"But didn't Tommy Fox make a joke?" Jolly Robin asked.

"A very poor one!" old Mr. Crow replied. "A very poor joke, indeed!... I see," he added, "I see you've not had much experience laughing for people. And here's where you make a mistake. You laugh at other people's jokes, which is all wrong. After this you must laugh at my jokes — do you understand?"

Jolly Robin said he understood. And Mr. Crow remarked that he was glad there would be no more trouble.

12

"And now," the old fellow said, "now we'll go over to the swamp, where Uncle Sammy Coon lives. We ought to have some fun with him."

So over to the swamp they flew, where they found Uncle Sammy Coon sunning himself in the top of a tall hemlock.

"How-dy-do!" said Mr. Crow.

But Uncle Sammy Coon did not answer.

"We're in luck!" Mr. Crow said with a chuckle. "I declare, I believe the old beggar's asleep. Just watch me play a practical joke on him!"

So Mr. Crow lighted on a branch near Uncle Sammy Coon and began tickling his nose.

Pretty soon Uncle Sammy Coon sneezed. And when that happened, Mr. Crow jumped back quickly. But Uncle Sammy didn't awake — at least, he didn't open his eyes. So Mr. Crow tickled his nose again.

Now, old Mr. Crow was so amused that he glanced at Jolly Robin, to see if he was watching. And in that instant when Mr. Crow looked away, Uncle Sammy Coon leaped at him. He caught Mr. Crow by the tail, too.

The old gentleman set up a great din. He squawked, "Help! help!" at the top of his voice and flapped his broad wings.

The struggle was over in a moment. By a great effort Mr. Crow broke away, leaving one of his tail-feathers with Uncle Sammy Coon, and flew into another tree near-by.

Then Jolly Robin laughed as if he would never stop. He thought that it must be the proper time to laugh, because Mr. Crow had said he was going to play a joke on Uncle Sammy.

Mr. Crow, however, seemed to think differently about the matter.

"Do keep quiet!" he cried. "There's nothing to laugh at, so far as I can see."

"But you said you were going to play a joke on Uncle Sammy Coon, didn't you?" Jolly inquired.

"Yes!" Mr. Crow replied. "But it's no joke to lose a tail-feather. And I wouldn't think of laughing at what just happened.... Besides," he continued, "your laughter is altogether wrong. What you must try to do is to laugh very sadly. In fact," he added, "I wouldn't mind if you shed a few tears, because I feel quite upset over this unfortunate accident."

Well, Jolly Robin saw at once that it was impossible for him to please Mr. Crow.

"My laughter," he said, "is always merry. I couldn't laugh sadly, no matter how hard I might try. And as for shedding tears, I couldn't weep for you even if you lost all your tail-feathers, Mr. Crow."

"Then you may leave at once!" Mr. Crow cried, just as if Farmer Green's pasture belonged to him.

"Yes!" Jolly Robin answered. "I may — and then again, I may not!"

And since he stayed right there and laughed, old Mr. Crow himself flew away. It was a long while, too, before he could bear to hear people laugh. For he thought they must be laughing at him, because he had lost a tail-feather.

And perhaps that was what amused Jolly Robin, though I never thought of that before.

VII

A NEW WAY TO TRAVEL

The time had come when Jolly Robin was ready to begin his long journey to the South, for it was growing quite cold. On some days there was no sun at all. And even when the weather was fair the sun rose late and went to bed early. It was exactly the sort of weather Jolly Robin did not like.

"No doubt you'll be leaving us soon," Jasper Jay remarked to Jolly one day, when the two chanced to meet in Farmer Green's woods, where the beeches grew.

"I expect to start to-morrow," Jolly Robin answered with a short laugh. The mere thought of his warm, light-flooded winter home in the Southland made him feel glad.

"Well, well!" Jasper Jay exclaimed. "I'm glad I happened to see you, for I know of a new way to travel."

And Jolly Robin wanted to know all about it.

"If it's a better way than the old, I'll be pleased to try it," he said.

"Oh! it's much better," Jasper told him. "If I hadn't made up my mind to spend the winter in Pleasant Valley, I'd go the new way myself. But the beechnut crop is good this fall. So I shall stay right here to enjoy it."

"Tell me how we're to go, if you please!" Jolly Robin urged him.

"We?" said Jasper. "You don't mean to say you are going with a crowd, do you?"

"Why, yes!" Jolly Robin replied. "All the Robins are leaving to-morrow. And I had intended to go with them."

Jasper Jay shook his head.

"Take my advice and don't do any such thing," he said. "You'll find it quieter travelling alone. And though you may not know it, it's the fashionable thing to do."

Jolly Robin laughed when Jasper said that.

"But I'm not a fashionable person!" he exclaimed.

"Then you should become one," Jasper told him. "Besides, the new way is easier, as well as more stylish. But if you're afraid to try something new, of course I wouldn't think of urging you."

"I'm not afraid!" Jolly Robin cried. "And if you'll only tell me what I'm to do, I promise you I'll do it!"

"Good!" said Jasper Jay. "Meet me here day after to-morrow and I'll start you on your journey. I can't explain anything now, because I must hurry over to the woods at once, where my cousin, Mr. Crow, is waiting for me." Then he flew away, screaming a loud good-by as he went.

So Jolly Robin hastened back to the orchard, to find his wife and tell her what he had decided to do.

He had no difficulty at all in finding her. But he had no end of trouble trying to persuade her to travel with him the new way, instead of going along with the crowd in the good, old-fashioned style. In fact, she raised so many objections, saying how lonely it would be and how dangerous it was to travel in a small party and that she didn't want to be fashionable—she raised so many objections that at last Jolly Robin said very well! she might do as she pleased. But as for him, he was going to meet Jasper Jay just as he had promised. And since the new way was easier, he expected to reach their winter home long before she arrived, even if he did start a day later.

But he was disappointed, all the same. And he kept up such a constant laughing and joking all the rest of that day that his wife knew he must be feeling quite out of sorts.

For that was a way Jolly Robin had. The worse he felt, the happier he always acted. And it was not a bad way, either.

VIII

JOLLY IS LEFT BEHIND

All of Jolly Robin's friends and relations were greatly surprised when they saw him bidding his wife and children good-by, on the day the Robin family started from Pleasant Valley for their winter home in the South.

"What's this?" they cried. "Aren't you coming with us?"

And Jolly Robin laughed and said to them gaily:

"Not to-day! But you'll find me waiting for you when you reach your journey's end."

His wife, however, shook her head.

"It's one of his queer notions — his and Jasper Jay's," she explained.

"Tut, tut!" her husband said. And he chucked her under the chin — and winked at his friends.

There was no time to say anything more, for everyone was eager to start. So the travellers called good-by to Jolly, while he waved a farewell to them.

It was not many minutes before he was the only member of the Robin family left in Pleasant Valley. He felt very lonely, all at once. And he wanted to hurry after the others. But he knew what Jasper Jay would say, if he did. Jasper would be sure to tell people that Jolly Robin was afraid to travel a new way.... Of course, Jolly didn't want that to be said about him. So he looked as cheerful as he could; and he whistled the merriest tune he knew. Nobody — except his wife, maybe — would have guessed that he wasn't perfectly happy.

Jolly spent a very lonely night. When he went to the roost where the whole Robin family had been sleeping for several weeks, he found it distressingly silent, after the gay chatter that he had grown accustomed to hearing there. And try as he would, he could not keep just a hint of sadness out of his good-night song.

But in the morning he felt better. And he welcomed the dawn with a carol that was joyous enough for anybody. For this was the day when Jasper Jay was going to show him the new way to travel. Yes! he, too, would soon be hurrying southwards, where the sun was warm.

It was no wonder that he sang, "Cheerily-cheerup, cheerily-cheerup," right merrily.

As soon as he had eaten his breakfast, Jolly went to the place where the beeches grew, to find Jasper Jay. And Jasper was there, just finishing his own breakfast. But he was too busy, he said, to bother with Jolly Robin just then.

"You meet me in the orchard this afternoon," he said, "when the sun's over the mountain, and I'll start you on your journey."

So Jolly Robin had to wait all the long day, while Jasper Jay did a hundred silly things, such as mocking Farmer Green's cat, and teasing a sleepy young owl, and making the woods echo with his hoarse screams. Jasper was late, too, in keeping his appointment in the orchard. Jolly Robin waited for him until almost sunset before Jasper Jay appeared. But Jolly was so glad to see Jasper that he never once thought of being angry with him.

"Come along!" said the blue-coated rascal. "Follow me and you'll soon learn the new way to the South. And if it isn't a good one I hope I'll never eat another beechnut."

Jolly Robin laughed. He was sure, then, that he had nothing to worry about. For everybody knew that Jasper Jay was specially fond of beechnuts.

IX

JOLLY'S MISTAKE

With Jolly Robin following close behind him, Jasper Jay flew directly to the crossroads, almost half-way to the village. Once there, he perched himself upon the sign-post at the four corners. And Jolly Robin seated himself upon one of the boards that were nailed to the post.

"Here we are!" said Jasper Jay. "You see how easy it is."

"When will the post begin to move?" Jolly Robin inquired, a bit anxiously. He had waited a whole day to begin his long journey to the South, so it was only natural that he should want to start at once.

"What's that you say?" asked Jasper Jay. And when Jolly repeated his question, Jasper began to scream with laughter. "Well, that's a good one!" he said at last. "So you thought the post was going to pull itself out of the ground and fly away with you, did you?"

"Why, yes!" Jolly Robin replied. "Aren't these wings?" he asked, looking down at the boards. "They're already spread," he observed.

It was some minutes before Jasper Jay could answer him, for he was laughing again. But finally he managed to speak.

"Those aren't wings!" he cried. "They're sign-boards, to tell you which road to take. Of course, you can't expect to read a sign when you're sitting on it. Just go over to the fence across the road and you can see the sign that you're on now."

So Jolly Robin fluttered over to the fence. And from there he could see the sign-board plainly. This is what it looked like:

TO SKY POND, 15 MILES

"There!" Jasper Jay cried, when Jolly had read the sign aloud. "You see how easy it is. All you need do is to follow this road to which the hand points."

"Then I shall have to fly, after all," Jolly Robin said. He had expected to have a ride. And naturally he was disappointed. Then he read the sign once more. "Sky Pond!" he exclaimed. "I don't want to go to Sky Pond. I want to go to the South!"

"Well, Sky Pond's south of Pleasant Valley," Jasper Jay explained. "It's right on your way to your winter home. And all you have to do when you reach Sky Pond will be to find another sign, which ought to say something like this: 'To the South, one thousand miles.' You see how simple it is," Jasper Jay remarked. "With a sign-board to guide you, you can't go wrong."

But it seemed to Jolly that the new way of travelling was far more difficult than the old. He said as much to Jasper Jay, too. "I wish--" he added - "I wish I had started yesterday, with the others."

At that Jasper Jay said, "Nonsense!" And he muttered something about dunces, and mollycoddles, and - yes! 'fraid-cats!

Perhaps Jasper hadn't intended that Jolly Robin should hear those words - and perhaps he had. Anyhow, he was sorry afterward that he had spoken so loud. For the first thing he knew, Jolly Robin flew straight at him with shrill chirps of rage. And Jasper was so surprised - and frightened, too - that he flew off as fast as he could go, following the road that led to Sky Pond, fifteen miles away, with Jolly Robin after him.

Jolly chased him for a long time, until at last Jasper Jay swerved to one side and turned toward home.

But Jolly Robin followed him no longer. He kept straight on, and on, and on. And he flew so fast and so far before he stopped that he overtook the party that had started a whole day ahead of him.

So he travelled to his winter home in the old-fashioned way, after all. And though Jolly Robin laughed when he told his friends about Jasper Jay's new style of travelling, there was one thing over which he could not smile, even then.

You see, "'fraid-cat" was a name he couldn't abide.

X

THE WHITE GIANT

It was a raw March day when Jolly Robin returned to Pleasant Valley one spring. There had just been a heavy fall of snow—big, wet flakes which Farmer Green called "sugar-snow," though it was no sweeter than any other. Johnnie Green liked that kind of snow because it made the best snowballs. And he had had a fine time playing in the orchard near the farmhouse, not long before Jolly Robin appeared there.

Now, the orchard was the place where Jolly Robin and his wife had had their nest the summer before. So it was natural that he should want to go there at once and look about a bit.

He perched himself on a bare limb, where he sang "Cheerily-cheerup" a few times, in spite of the snow and the cold, whistling wind. He knew that the weather would grow warmer soon; and he was glad to be in Pleasant Valley once more, though he had to confess to himself that he liked the orchard better when the grass was green and the trees were gay with apple-blossoms.

"It's really a beautiful place for a home," he told himself. "I don't wonder that Farmer Green likes to live near the orchard. And now I'll just go over to the house and see if I can't get a peep at him and his wife and his boy, Johnnie—and the hired-man, too."

So Jolly Robin jumped off the bough and started through the frosty air toward the farmhouse. But all at once he saw a sight that sent him darting into a tree. He hid there for a while and something made him shiver— something besides the cold wind.

Yes! Jolly Robin was the least bit frightened. For he had caught a glimpse of a strange man. It was neither Farmer Green nor his hired-man, for this was a giant. He had big, black eyes and a great lump of a nose, which stuck out queerly from his pale moon-face. He was dressed all in white, except for a battered, old, black hat, which he wore tipped over one eye. In one hand he held a stick. And it seemed to Jolly Robin that the queer man was just about to hurl it at something.

In spite of his uneasiness, Jolly peeped around his tree and watched the stranger. But he did not throw the stick. He stood quite still and seemed to be waiting. And Jolly Robin waited, too, and stared at him.

"Maybe there's a squirrel hiding behind a tree," he said to himself. "Perhaps this man in white is going to throw the stick as soon as the squirrel shows himself."

But no squirrel appeared. And Jolly Robin was just about to start for the farmhouse again when he saw somebody pop out of the woodshed door and come running toward the orchard.

"Here's Johnnie Green!" Jolly exclaimed. He knew Johnnie at once, because neither Farmer Green nor the hired-man ever went hopping and skipping about like that.

Pretty soon Jolly saw Johnnie Green stop and make an armful of snowballs. And then he went straight toward the stranger in white. Though Johnnie began to shout, the man in white did not even turn his head. And then Johnnie Green shied a snowball at him.

The snowball sailed through the air and struck the stranger's battered hat, knocking it off into the snow. And, of course, Jolly Robin couldn't help laughing. He was more surprised than ever, too, because the moon-faced man did not move even then. Anyone else would have wheeled about and chased Johnnie Green. But this odd gentleman didn't seem to know that his hat had been knocked off.

"That's queer!" said Jolly Robin to himself. "He must be asleep. But I should think he would wake up."

While Jolly was wondering, Johnnie Green threw another snowball. And when it struck the stranger a very peculiar thing happened.

And Jolly Robin did not laugh. He was too frightened to do anything but gasp.

XI

WHAT A SNOWBALL DID

Jolly Robin was too frightened to laugh when he saw Johnnie Green's second snowball strike the moon-faced stranger in the orchard. You see, the snowball hit one of the stranger's arms. And to Jolly's amazement, the arm at once dropped off and dashed upon the ground, breaking into a dozen pieces.

That alone was enough to startle Jolly Robin. But the moon-faced man paid not the slightest attention to the accident. There was something ghostly in the way he stood there, all in white, never moving, never once saying a word.

But Johnnie Green did not seem frightened at all. He set up a great shouting and began to let fly his snowballs as fast as he could throw them.

They did not all find the mark. But the very last one struck the silent stranger squarely upon his left ear. And to Jolly Robin's horror, his head toppled off and fell horridly at his feet.

Jolly Robin fully expected the man in white to turn and chase Johnnie Green then — or at least to hurl his stick at Johnnie. But nothing of the sort happened. And Jolly did not wait for anything more. He felt that he had seen quite enough. So he flew away to the shelter of the woods, to find somebody to whom he could talk and tell of the strange thing that had happened in the orchard.

Over in the woods Jolly was lucky enough to meet Jimmy Rabbit, who was always very friendly toward him. And as soon as he had inquired about Jimmy Rabbit's health (they had not seen each other since the previous fall, you know), Jolly related how he had seen Johnnie Green knock off the head of the man in the orchard.

"And the man never paid the slightest heed to what happened," said Jolly Robin. "He had a stick in his hand; but he didn't throw it."

"There's nothing queer about that," Jimmy Rabbit remarked. "How could he see where to throw his stick, when he had no head?"

But Jolly Robin could not answer that question. And he looked more puzzled than ever.

"I don't understand it," he said with a shake of his own head. "The whole affair was very odd. I'm afraid I shall not care to live in the orchard this summer, especially if there's a headless man there! For how can he ever see to leave the orchard?"

It was Jimmy Rabbit's turn to look puzzled, for that was a question that he couldn't answer.

"Maybe there is something queer about this case," he said. "I'll go over to the orchard to-morrow and take a look at that headless stranger and see what I think about him. If you'll meet me here we can go together."

Now, Jolly Robin had almost decided that he would never go near the orchard again. But he felt that if he went with Jimmy Rabbit there ought not to be much danger. So he agreed to Jimmy's suggestion.

"I'll be here before the morning's gone," he promised.

XII

JOLLY FEELS BETTER

Jolly Robin awoke at dawn. And he knew at once that the day was going to be a fine one. Though the sun had not yet peeped above the rim of the eastern hills, Jolly Robin was sure that there would be plenty of sunshine a little later. He had many ways of his own for telling the weather; and he never made a mistake about it.

Now, it had grown quite warm by the time Jolly Robin went to the woods late in the morning to meet Jimmy Rabbit. And the snow had melted away as if by magic.

"Summer's coming! Summer's coming!" Jolly called joyfully as soon as Jimmy Rabbit came hopping into sight. "The apple-blossoms will burst out before we know it."

"Yes—and the cabbages, too," Jimmy Rabbit replied. "I'm glad the white giant in the orchard lost his head," he added, "because there's no telling what he would have done to the cabbages later, if he had wandered into the garden. He might have eaten every one of them. And I shouldn't have liked that very well."

Then they started off together toward the orchard to look at the headless stranger who had given Jolly Robin such a fright the day before. Jimmy Rabbit went bounding along with great leaps, while Jolly Robin flew above him and tried not to go too fast for his long-eared friend.

Once in the orchard, Jolly led Jimmy to the spot where he had seen Johnnie Green knock off the giant's head with the snowball.

"Here he is!" Jolly Robin whispered—for he was still somewhat afraid of the giant, in spite of his having lost his head. "He doesn't seem as big as he was yesterday. And he has dropped the stick that he carried."

Jimmy Rabbit stopped short in his tracks and stared at the still figure under the apple tree. For a few moments he did not speak.

"That looks to me like snow," he said at last. And he crept up to what was left of the giant and sniffed at him. "It is snow!" he declared.

When he heard that, Jolly Robin flew to a low branch just above the giant.

"I don't understand it," he said. "There's his head on the ground, with the big, black eyes. They certainly aren't made of snow."

"No!" Jimmy Rabbit agreed, as he sniffed at the terrible eyes. "They're butternuts—that's what they are!"

Well, Jolly Robin was so surprised that he all but tumbled off his perch.

"There's his hat—" he continued, as he clung to the limb—"that's a real hat. It's not made of snow—or butternuts, either."

"Yes!" Jimmy Rabbit said. "It's a sure-enough hat. Farmer Green wore it on Sundays for a good many years. I've often seen him starting for the meeting-house over the hill with this very hat on his head."

"Then the giant stole it from him!" Jolly Robin cried in great excitement.

But Jimmy Rabbit thought differently.

"It's my opinion—" he said—"it's my opinion that Johnnie Green took this old hat and put it on the giant's head, after he had made him."

"Made him!" Jolly Robin repeated. "You don't mean to say that Johnnie Green could make a giant, do you?"

"Well, he knows how to make a snow-man—so I've been told," Jimmy Rabbit replied. "And though I've never seen one before, it's plain that that's what this creature is."

Jolly Robin had listened with growing wonder. Spending his winters in the South, as he did, he had never even heard of a snow-man.

"Are they dangerous—these snow-men?" he inquired anxiously.

"This one certainly isn't," Jimmy Rabbit told him. "With his head off, he can't do any harm. And with the sun shining so warm I should say that by to-morrow he'll be gone for good. It looks to me as if he might be the last snow-man of the winter, for I don't believe there'll be any more snow until next fall."

"Good!" Jolly Robin cried. "I shall come back to the orchard to live, after all, just as I had intended." And he felt so happy that he began to sing.

"I'm glad I brought you here to see the snow giant," he told Jimmy Rabbit, when he had finished his song. "But when my wife and I start to build our summer-house a little later in the spring, I hope you'll say nothing to her about this affair. It might upset her, you know, if she knew that a giant lost his head in the orchard—even if he was made of snow."

"I understand!" said Jimmy Rabbit. "And I won't mention the matter to her. You're afraid she might lose her head, I suppose, if she heard about it."

Having made a joke, Jimmy Rabbit thought it was a good time for him to be leaving. So he said good-by and hopped briskly away.

And Jolly Robin's wife never knew that her husband and Jimmy Rabbit had a secret that they did not tell her.

Of course, if they had told her it would have been no secret at all.

XIII

THE HERMIT

Though Jolly Robin was quite bold for his size, he had a cousin who was actually shy. This timid relation of Jolly's belonged to the Hermit Thrush family; and Jolly Robin always spoke of him as "The Hermit," which was a good name for him, because he never strayed from the depths of the swamp near Black Creek. At least, he stayed there all summer long, until the time came for him to go South.

If Jolly Robin wanted to see this shy cousin, he had to go into the swamp. For the Hermit never repaid any of Jolly's calls. He was afraid of Farmer Green and the other people that lived in the farmhouse. Apple orchards, and gardens and open fields he considered good places to avoid, because he thought them dangerous.

"There's no place to live that's quite as safe and pleasant as a swamp," he often remarked. "I have one brother who prefers an evergreen thicket, which doesn't make a bad home. And another brother of mine lives in some bushes near a road. But how he can like such a dwelling-place as that is more than I can understand."

Now, there were two things for which this cousin of Jolly Robin's was noted. He was an exquisite singer; and he always wore a fine, spotted waistcoat.

Jolly always admired the Hermit's singing. But he didn't like his spotted waistcoat at all.

"That cousin of mine is too much of a dandy," Jolly remarked to his wife one day. "I'm going to pay him a visit this afternoon. And I shall speak to him about that waistcoat he's so fond of wearing. It's well enough for city birds to dress in such finery. But it's a foppish thing for anybody to wear way up here in the country."

Jolly's wife told him plainly that he had better mind his own business.

"It's no affair of yours," she said. "And you ought not to mention the matter to your cousin."

Jolly Robin did not answer her. He thought there was no use arguing with his wife. And since the Hermit was his own cousin, he saw no reason why he shouldn't tell his relation exactly what he thought.

The Hermit appeared glad to see Jolly Robin when he came to the swamp that afternoon. At least, the Hermit said he was much pleased. He had very polished manners for a person that lived in a swamp. Beside him, Jolly Robin seemed somewhat awkward and clownish. But then, Jolly always claimed that he was just a plain, rough-and-ready countryman.

"I never put on any airs," he often said. "Farmer Green and I are a good deal alike in that respect."

After the Hermit had inquired about Jolly's health, and that of his wife as well, he smoothed down his spotted vest, flicked a bit of moss off his tail, and said that if Jolly cared to hear him he would sing one of his best songs.

"I'd like to hear you sing!" Jolly told him.

So the Hermit sang a very sweet and tender melody, which was quite different from Jolly's cheery carols.

It was a great pleasure to hear such a beautiful song. And Jolly Robin was so delighted that he began to laugh heartily the moment his cousin had finished the final note.

"I wouldn't laugh, if I were you," the Hermit reproved him mildly. "That's a sad song.... If you care to weep, I'd be more than gratified," he said. And he shuddered slightly, because Jolly's boisterous laughter grated upon his sensitive nerves.

You can see, just from that, that the Hermit was a very different person from his merry cousin, Jolly Robin.

XIV

ONE OR TWO BLUNDERS

Jolly Robin's cousin, the Hermit, seemed much disappointed because Jolly did not weep after hearing the beautiful, sad song. But no matter how mournful a song might be, Jolly Robin could no more have shed tears over it than a fish could have. Naturally, a fish never weeps, because it would be a silly thing to do. Surrounded by water as he is, a fish could never see his own tears. And so all the weeping he might do would be merely wasted.

Not wanting to hurt his cousin's feelings, Jolly Robin said that he would try to weep after he went home. And that made the Hermit feel happier once more.

"Perhaps you'd like to see our eggs?" he suggested.

And since Jolly Robin said he would be delighted to look at them, if the Hermit's wife had no objection, his cousin led him further into the swamp. And there, in a nest of moss and leaves, lined with pine needles, the Hermit proudly pointed to three greenish blue eggs, somewhat smaller than those in Jolly's own nest in Farmer Green's orchard.

Jolly Robin stared at the nest in amazement. And pretty soon the Hermit grew quite uncomfortable.

"What's the matter?" he asked. "You seem surprised."

"I certainly am!" Jolly Robin cried. "How do you dare do it?"

"Do what?" his cousin inquired uneasily.

"Why, you and your wife have built your nest on the ground!"

"Well, why shouldn't we?" the Hermit asked. And he looked the least bit angry.

"But everybody knows that the best place for a nest is in a tree," Jolly Robin told him.

His cousin shook his head at that.

"It's a matter of taste," he said. "Our family have always preferred to build their nests on the ground. And as for me, I shall continue to follow their example.... It suits me very well," he added.

Jolly Robin couldn't help laughing, the sight struck him as being such an odd one.

"It's a wonder—" he remarked—"it's a wonder your wife doesn't bury her eggs in the sand beside the creek, like old Mrs. Turtle."

"I'd thank you," said the Hermit, stiffly, "not to say such things about my wife." And though he spoke politely enough, his manner was quite cold. It was clear that he felt terribly insulted.

Jolly Robin saw that he had blundered. And wishing to change the subject, he said hastily:

"Won't you sing another song?"

So the Hermit cleared his throat and began to sing again.

Although this song was not so sad as the first one, Jolly Robin did not like it half so well. The chorus, especially, he considered quite offensive. And it is not surprising, perhaps, that it displeased him, for this is the way it went:

"Any old vest

May do for the rest;

But I like a spotted one best!"

If it hadn't been for that song, Jolly Robin would not have remembered that he had intended to speak to his cousin about his spotted waistcoat. Jolly had been so interested in the nest on the ground that the matter of the waistcoat had slipped out of his mind. But now he suddenly recalled the reason why he had come to see the Hermit. And he disliked his cousin's spotted finery more than ever.

Thereupon, he resolved that he would speak about it, too.

XV

LOST — A COUSIN!

When the Hermit Thrush had finished his song about the spotted vest, he looked at his cousin Jolly Robin out of the corner of his eye.

"How do you like that one?" he inquired. He noticed that Jolly was not laughing.

"That seems to me to be a very silly song," Jolly Robin said. "But I'm glad you sang it, because it has reminded me that I was going to speak to you about that spotted waistcoat you're so fond of wearing."

"What's the matter with my waistcoat?" the Hermit asked quickly. "I'm sure it's a very handsome one."

"I don't like it!" Jolly told him. "I wouldn't be caught with it on me for anything. Everybody says that you're a great dandy because you wear it. And since you're my cousin, I think I ought to tell you what people are saying about you."

"I don't care what people say!" the Hermit exclaimed. "Those that don't like my beautiful waistcoat can look the other way when I'm around. And if my style of dress doesn't please you, I'd suggest that you keep out of this swamp."

"Now, don't get angry!" Jolly Robin begged. He gave his cousin a smile, hoping that it might make him feel pleasanter. "I was only trying to help you. I was only going to advise you to wear a red waistcoat, like mine."

Now, the mere thought of wearing a red waistcoat made the Hermit feel faint. Some people say that all great singers are like that. If they don't like a thing, they can't bear even to think about it. And it was a fact that the words "red waistcoat" had always made Jolly Robin's cousin shudder.

Maybe one reason why he never went to visit Jolly was because he couldn't endure the sight of his bright red vest.

Of course, Jolly Robin knew nothing about all this.

"Red would be very becoming to you," he continued. "And it's certainly a cheerful color, too. You need brightening up. I don't believe it's good for you, living in this damp swamp and singing sad songs. What you ought to do is to get some clothes like mine and bring your wife over to Farmer Green's orchard and build a nest in an apple tree.... We could have some gay times together," he said smilingly.

Like many other people Jolly Robin thought his own ways were the best. And since the Hermit was just as sure that nobody else knew how to dress, or how to sing, or how to build a house as well as he did, it is quite plain that the two cousins never could agree.

"Just tell your wife about my plan when she comes home," said Jolly Robin. "And I'll fly over to-morrow and show you the way to the orchard."

"I'll tell her," his cousin promised.

"Good!" said Jolly Robin. And he gave his delicate cousin a hearty slap on the back, which made the poor fellow wince—for it hurt him not a little. "Good-by!" Jolly cried. And chirping loudly, he flew back home.

Now, Jolly noticed, as he left, that his cousin called "Farewell!" in a melancholy tone. But he thought no more about it at the time. He told his wife the good news as soon as he reached the orchard; for Jolly was sure that his cousin the Hermit was going to follow his advice.

But the next day Jolly met with a great surprise. When he went to the swamp near Black Creek he couldn't find his cousin anywhere—nor his cousin's wife, either. Even their three eggs had disappeared from the nest on the ground.

"I hope Fatty Coon hasn't eaten the eggs," said Jolly Robin, as he gazed into the empty nest. "But it's no more than anybody could expect who's so foolish as to build a nest on the ground." He grew quite uneasy. And he was puzzled, too.

Later, when Jolly Robin met old Mr. Crow, he learned that his cousin, the Hermit Thrush, and his wife had moved away from the swamp the evening before.

"They've left for parts unknown," old Mr. Crow explained. "I saw them when they started. And when I asked your cousin where they were going, he said that they didn't know, but they were hoping to find some peaceful neighborhood where they had no relations."

"That's strange!" Jolly Robin exclaimed. "We are very fond of each other — my cousin and I. By the way," he added, "did you happen to notice what sort of waistcoat he was wearing?"

Mr. Crow said he had noticed; and that it was a light-colored one with dark spots.

"Dear me!" said Jolly Robin. "I was hoping he had put on a red one. But since he moved in such a hurry, perhaps he hadn't time to change."

Whether that was the case, Jolly Robin never learned. For he never saw his cousin the Hermit again.

XVI

JEALOUS JASPER JAY

The feathered folk in Pleasant Valley were all aflutter. They had heard a strange tale—the oddest tale, almost, that had ever been told in their neighborhood.

It was Jolly Robin who had started the story. And since he was not in the habit of playing jokes on people, everybody believed what he said—at least, everybody except Jasper Jay. He declared from the first that Jolly Robin's tale was a hoax.

"I claim that there's not a word of truth in it!" Jasper Jay said.

Now, there was a reason why Jasper spoke in that disagreeable way. He didn't want the story to be true. And, somehow, he felt that if he said it was a hoax, it would really prove to be one.

"I know well enough," said Jasper, "that there's no golden bird in Pleasant Valley—and nowhere else, either!"

You see, Jolly Robin had hurried to the woods one day and told everyone he met that a wonderful golden bird had come to Pleasant Valley.

"He's not just yellow, like a goldfinch. He's solid gold all over, from the tip of his bill to the tip of his tail. Even his feet are golden. And he glistens in the sunshine as if he were afire!" That was the way Jolly Robin described the marvellous newcomer. "He's the handsomest bird that ever was seen," he added.

Perhaps Jasper Jay was jealous. You know he was a great dandy, being very proud of his blue suit, which was really quite beautiful. Anyhow, Jasper Jay began to sulk as soon as he heard the news.

"Where is this magnificent person?" he asked Jolly Robin with a sneer. "Do let me see him! And if he wants to fight, I'll soon spoil his finery for him. He won't look so elegant after I've pulled out his tail-feathers."

But Jolly Robin wouldn't tell anybody where he had seen the wonderful bird. He said the golden bird was three times as big as Jasper Jay. And he didn't want Jasper to get hurt, even if he was so disagreeable.

Anyone can see, just from that, that Jolly Robin was very kind.

"You'd better be careful, or I'll fight you, too!" Jasper warned him.

But Jolly was not afraid. He knew that Jasper was something of a braggart and a bully. He had chased Jasper once. And he thought he could do it again, if he had to.

"My cousin will tell me where to find this yellow fellow," said Jasper Jay at last. "There's not much that happens in Pleasant Valley that my cousin doesn't know about." So he flew off to find old Mr. Crow—for he was the cousin of whom Jasper was speaking.

Jasper found Mr. Crow in his favorite tree in the pine woods. And sure enough! the old gentleman seemed to know all about the golden bird. But like Jolly Robin, he refused to say where he had seen him. To tell the truth, Mr. Crow had never set eyes on the strange bird. But he did not like to admit it. "He's a great credit to the neighborhood," said old Mr. Crow. "And you'd better let him alone, if you should happen to find him, because he's solid gold, you know. And if you flew at him and tried to peck him, just as likely as not you'd break your bill on him, he's so hard."

Old Mr. Crow's warning, however, had no effect at all upon Jasper Jay.

"I'm going to search every corner in the valley until I find this fop. And I'll teach him that he'd better get out of our neighborhood with his fine airs."

When he heard that, old Mr. Crow shook his head.

"You're going to have trouble!" he told Jasper. And then he hurried away to tell Jolly Robin that he ought to advise the golden bird to leave Pleasant Valley.

But Jolly Robin said he had not spoken with the stranger. And never having talked with a golden bird, he felt a bit shy about saying anything to him.

"Then there'll be a terrible fight, I'm afraid," said Mr. Crow.

"I'm afraid so," Jolly Robin agreed. And strange as it may seem, they both said that if there was going to be a fight they didn't want to miss seeing it.

XVII

ONLY A ROOSTER

Jasper Jay spent several days looking for the great golden bird that Jolly Robin had described. But Jasper couldn't find the wonderful creature anywhere. And he was wondering if it wasn't just a hoax after all, as he had claimed. He had almost decided to give up his search, when he chanced to meet Bennie Barn-Swallow one day. Jasper happened to mention that he was on the lookout for Jolly Robin's strange bird; and Bennie Barn-Swallow said quickly:

"Do you mean the bird of gold?"

"The bird of brass, I should say!" Jasper replied, with his nose in the air. "You haven't seen him, have you?"

"Why, yes!" said Bennie. "He stays right near my house."

Of course, Jasper Jay knew that Bennie lived in a mud house, under the eaves of Farmer Green's barn. So he cried at once: "Then my search is ended! I'll come over to the barn this afternoon and fight the upstart."

The news spread quickly—the news of the fight that was going to take place at Farmer Green's barn. And as soon as he heard it, Jolly Robin went straight to the barn and asked the golden bird if he wouldn't leave Pleasant Valley at once.

But the great, gorgeous creature paid no attention to Jolly Robin's request. Indeed, he seemed not to hear his words at all—though Jolly Robin thought the stranger was just pretending.

Jolly had to sing a good many songs that day to keep up his spirits. Somehow, he felt that it was all his fault that there was going to be a fight.

"I wish I hadn't told anyone about the golden bird," he said. "Maybe he would have flown away before Jasper Jay heard of his being here."

Well, Jasper invited everybody to come to the barn late in the afternoon to see him whip the golden bird and pull out his tail-feathers.

"There's going to be some fun," said Jasper Jay. "Nobody ought to miss it."

So, as the afternoon waned, the feathered folk began to gather in the orchard. Jolly Robin was there, and his wife, and old Mr. Crow, Rusty Wren, Bobbie Bobolink, Miss Kitty Catbird, and a good many others as well. There was a good deal of noise, for everyone was chattering. And Jasper Jay made almost as great a din as all his friends together. He boasted in a loud voice that he was going to give the golden bird a terrible beating. And he was so pleased with himself that some of his companions whispered to one another that it might be a good thing if the golden bird gave Jasper a sound whipping.

At last Jasper Jay called out that he was ready. And then he started for Farmer Green's barn, while the eager crew followed close behind him. They all alighted on the ridge of the barn. And like Jasper Jay, they sat there for a short time and stared at the golden bird, who shimmered like fire in the slanting rays of the setting sun.

Jolly Robin and Bennie Barn-Swallow had seen him before; so they weren't surprised. But all the others gazed at him in amazement.

Now, to Jasper Jay the golden bird looked enormous. He was perched high up on a rod which rose above the roof. And he seemed very proud and disdainful. In fact, he paid no attention at all to the curious flock that watched him.

For a little while nobody said a word. And Jasper Jay was the first to speak.

"Fiddlesticks!" he cried. "This is nothing but a barnyard fowl. He's a rooster — that's what he is!"

XVIII

ON TOP OF THE BARN

All the feathered folk on the roof of Farmer Green's barn saw at once that Jasper Jay had told the truth. The golden bird was a rooster, just as Jasper had said. But it seemed strange to them that a rooster should sit on so high a perch.

"It looks to me," said old Mr. Crow, "it looks to me as if he had flown up here and lighted on that rod and then was afraid to fly down again."

"I'll knock him off!" cried Jasper Jay. And he made ready to swoop at the stranger.

"I wouldn't do that!" said Jolly Robin.

"No!" Jasper Jay replied. "I know you wouldn't. You'd be afraid to do such a thing."

"It's not that," Jolly Robin told him, "though he is ten times my size. This is what I mean: He's a peaceable fellow. And though I will admit that he seems a little too proud, he hasn't harmed anybody. So why should anybody harm him?"

"He's a barnyard fowl and he belongs on the ground," Jasper Jay declared. "If we let him stay up here in the air there's no knowing what Farmer Green's fowls will do. All his hens and roosters—and he has a hundred of 'em—may take to flying about where they don't belong. This golden gentleman is setting them a bad example. And it is my duty to teach him a lesson."

Now, the real reason why Jasper wanted to knock the golden rooster off his high perch was because he was so handsome. Jasper's fine blue suit looked quite dull beside the golden dress of the stranger. And that was more than Jasper could stand.

"Here I go!" Jasper cried. And he left his friends and flew straight at the golden fowl.

Jasper struck the rooster such a hard blow that he spun around on his perch twice. But he didn't lose his balance. And he never said a single word.

"I'll pull out his tail-feathers this time!" Jasper squawked, as he darted at the stranger again. But Jasper had no luck at all. Though he pecked viciously at the tail of the golden rooster, he succeeded only in hurting his own bill.

Several times Jasper tried. But not one tail-feather came away. And some of the onlookers began to smile. Old Mr. Crow even guffawed aloud. But Jasper Jay pretended not to hear him.

"Don't you think we'd better go away?" Jolly Robin asked Jasper at last.

"I think you had better leave," Jasper screamed. He was very angry, because he knew that his friends were laughing at him. And instead of flying at the golden rooster again he made a swift attack on Jolly Robin.

Being angry, Jasper had forgotten that Jolly Robin's wife was present. And to the blue-coated rascal there seemed suddenly to be as many as six Jolly Robins, each one with a furious wife, too.

Jasper fought his hardest. But he was no match for them. Very soon he made for the woods; and as he flew away a blue tail-feather with a white tip floated down into the barnyard, where Johnnie Green had stood for some minutes, watching the strange sight on the roof of his father's barn.

Johnnie picked up the feather and stuck it in his hat. And when he told his father, later, how a big blue jay had tried to whip the new weather-vane and a pair of robins as well, Farmer Green threw back his head and laughed loudly.

"Don't you believe me?" Johnnie asked him. "Here's the blue jay's tail-feather, anyhow. And that ought to prove that I am telling the truth."

But Farmer Green only laughed all the more. You see, he could hardly believe all the strange things that happened in the neighborhood.

XIX

CURIOUS MR. CROW

Living in the orchard as they did, near the farmhouse, Jolly Robin and his wife knew more about Farmer Green's family than any of the other birds in Pleasant Valley, except maybe Rusty Wren. Being a house wren, Rusty was naturally on the best of terms with all the people in the farmhouse.

But all summer long Rusty Wren never strayed far from home. So it was Jolly Robin who told his friends in the woods many strange stories about what happened near the orchard. His account of the golden bird was only one of many curious tales that he related to the wondering wood-creatures.

Being so cheerful and having so much interesting news to tell, Jolly Robin was welcome wherever he went. And when his friends met him in the woods or the fields they were sure to stop and ask him if he hadn't some new story to tell. One day old Mr. Crow even took the trouble to fly all the way across the cornfield to the edge of the woods, where his sharp eyes had seen Jolly Robin eating wild cherries.

"I say, what do you know that's new?" Mr. Crow asked him. The old gentleman was a very curious person. Being a great gossip, he was always on the lookout for something to talk about.

"I don't believe I've seen anything lately that would interest you," Jolly replied, "unless it's the four-armed man."

Mr. Crow looked up quickly.

"What's that you say?" he exclaimed.

"The four-armed man!" Jolly Robin repeated.

"Is that a joke?" Mr. Crow asked. He was inclined to be suspicious, because he always disliked having tricks played upon him. "I've heard of—and seen—a two-headed calf," he remarked. "But a four-armed man is a little too much for me to believe in, unless I behold him with my own eyes."

Jolly Robin laughed.

"It's no joke at all!" he declared.

"Then what are you laughing at?" Mr. Crow inquired severely.

"Nothing!" Jolly Robin answered. "It's just a habit of mine to laugh."

"Very well!" said Mr. Crow. "I accept your apology. But please don't do it again.... And now," he added, "where, pray, is this wonderful four-armed man?"

"In the barnyard!" Jolly Robin informed him. "I've often seen him lately, walking between the house and the barn. He looks a good deal like the hired-man. But of course it can't be he, for the hired-man—as you yourself know—has but two arms."

"I must have a look at this monster," Mr. Crow remarked. "When would be a good time for me to see him?"

"At milking-time," Jolly Robin told him. "If you'll meet me on the bridge down the road when you see Johnnie Green and old dog Spot driving the cows home from the pasture this afternoon, I'll be glad to show you the four-armed man. And then you'll admit that I'm not joking."

"I'll certainly be there—" Mr. Crow promised—"but on one condition. You must tell me now whether you have ever known this queer being to fire a gun. If a two-armed man can shoot one gun, I see no reason why a four-armed man could not fire at least two guns at the same time. And if there's any chance of such a thing happening, I would not care to be present."

Jolly Robin had hard work to keep from laughing again. The very idea of the four-armed man aiming two guns at old Mr. Crow struck him as being very funny. He couldn't speak at all for a few moments. But he shook his head violently.

"You think there's no danger, then?" said Mr. Crow, anxiously.

"None at all!" Jolly Robin answered him. "He carries nothing more dangerous than milk-pails."

"Then I'll meet you on the bridge," Mr. Crow promised.

43

XX

THE FOUR-ARMED MAN

Old dog Spot was driving the last cow down the lane when Jolly Robin and Mr. Crow met on the bridge near the farmhouse, as they had agreed.

"Now, then—" said Mr. Crow, even before his broad wings had settled smoothly along his back—"now, then, where's the four-armed man?"

Jolly looked towards the barnyard.

"I don't see him yet," he said. "But he ought to appear any moment now. Let's move over to the big oak, for we can get a better view of the barnyard from the top of it."

Mr. Crow was more than willing. So they flew to the oak and waited for a time. They saw the cows file into the barn, each finding her own place in one of the two long rows of stanchions that faced each other across the wide aisle running the length of the barn. It was through that aisle that the men walked with great forkfuls of hay in the winter time, which they flung down before the cows, who munched it contentedly.

But it was summer now. And the cows found their own food in the pasture on the hillside. They came to the barn only to be milked.

"It's milking-time right now," Jolly Robin remarked. "And pretty soon you'll see the four-armed man come out of the barn with some pails full of milk. He'll carry them into the house, to set them in the buttery. We'll have a good look at him without his knowing anything about it."

And that was exactly what happened.

"Here he comes!" Jolly Robin exclaimed, as a figure stepped out of the barn and began walking toward the house. "Now, you'll have to admit that I wasn't joking when I told you the news of this strange being. You ought to be pretty glad I let you know about the four-armed man, Mr. Crow. I guess you never saw anything quite so queer as he is, even if you have seen a

44

two-headed calf." Jolly Robin said a great deal more to Mr. Crow. And he was so pleased that he started to sing a song.

But Mr. Crow quickly silenced him.

"Do keep still!" he whispered. "Do you want to get me into trouble? It's bad enough to have a trick like this played on me, without your making such a noise. Farmer Green might shoot me if he saw me so near his house. I thought—" Mr. Crow added—"I thought you laughed a little too much when you told me about your four-armed man. It's a hoax—a joke—a trick—and a very poor one, too."

Jolly Robin was puzzled enough by Mr. Crow's disagreeable remarks.

"I don't understand how you can say those things," he said.

Mr. Crow looked narrowly at his small companion before answering. And then he asked:

"Do you mean to say you never heard of a neck-yoke?"

"Never!" cried Jolly Robin.

"Well, well!" said Mr. Crow. "The ignorance of some people is more than I can understand.... That was no four-armed man. You said he looked like Farmer Green's hired-man; and it is not surprising that he does, for he is the hired-man. He has found an old neck-yoke somewhere. It is just a piece of wood that fits about his shoulders and around his neck and sticks out on each side of him like an arm. And he hooks a pail of milk to each end of the yoke, carrying his load in that way. I supposed," said Mr. Crow, "that people had stopped using neck-yokes fifty years ago. It's certainly that long since I've seen one."

"Then it's no wonder that I made a mistake!" Jolly Robin cried. "For I'm too young ever to have heard of a neck-yoke, even." And he laughed and chuckled merrily. "It's a good joke on me!" he said.

But old Mr. Crow did not laugh.

"There you go, making a noise again!" he said crossly. "A person's not safe in your company." And he hurried off across the meadow. Mr. Crow was always very nervous when he was near the farmhouse.

But Jolly Robin stayed right there until the hired-man walked back to the barn. He saw then that what Mr. Crow had told him was really so. And he never stopped laughing until long after sunset.

XXI

A DOLEFUL DITTY

Jolly Robin often complained about the wailing of Willie Whip-poor-will. Willie lived in the woods, which were not far from the orchard. And it was annoying to Jolly to hear his call, "Whip-poor-will, whip-poor-will," repeated over and over again for some two hours after Jolly's bed-time. Neither did Jolly Robin enjoy being awakened by that same sound an hour or two before he wanted to get up in the morning. And what was still worse, on moonlight nights Willie sometimes sang his favorite song from sunset to sunrise.

"What a doleful ditty!" said Jolly Robin. "I must see this fellow and tell him that he ought to change his tune." But the trouble was that Jolly Robin did not like to roam about at night. He was always too sleepy to do that. And in the daytime Willie Whip-poor-will was silent, resting or sleeping upon the ground in the woods.

But a day came at last when Jolly Robin stumbled upon Willie Whip-poor-will, sound asleep where he lived. And Jolly lost no time in waking him up.

"I've been wanting to speak to you for some time," he told the drowsy fellow.

"What's the matter?" Willie Whip-poor-will asked, with a startled stare. "Are the woods on fire?"

"No!" said Jolly Robin. "I want to talk with you — that's all." And he was as cheerful as anyone could have wished.

But Willie Whip-poor-will looked very cross.

"This is a queer time to make a call!" he grumbled. "I don't like to be disturbed in broad daylight. I supposed everybody knew that midnight is the proper time for a visit."

"But I'm always asleep then," Jolly Robin objected, "unless it's a moonlight night and you happen to be singing on my side of the woods."

47

Willie Whip-poor-will looked almost pleasant when Jolly said that.

"So you stay awake to hear me!" he exclaimed. "I see you like my singing."

Jolly Robin laughed, because Willie had made such a funny mistake.

"You're wrong!" he said. "In fact, I've been wanting to talk with you about that very thing. I want you to change your song, which is a very annoying one. It's altogether too disagreeable. I'll teach you my 'Cheerily-cheerup' song. You'll like it much better, I think. And I'm sure all your neighbors will.... Why not learn the new song right now?" Jolly asked.

But Willie Whip-poor-will made no answer. Looking at him more closely, Jolly Robin was amazed to see that he was sound asleep.

"Here, wake up!" Jolly cried, as he nudged Willie under a wing.

Again Willie Whip-poor-will sprang up with a bewildered expression.

"Hullo!" he said. "What's the trouble? Did a tree fall?"

"You went to sleep while I was talking to you," Jolly Robin explained.

"Oh!" said Willie Whip-poor-will. "That doesn't matter. You must be used to that." And the words were scarcely out of his mouth before he had fallen asleep again.

Jolly Robin looked at him in a puzzled way. He didn't see how he could teach Willie his "Cheerily-cheerup" song unless he could keep him awake. But he thought he ought to try; so he gave Willie a sharp tweak with his bill.

"Did you hear what I said about your singing?" he shouted right in Willie's ear.

Willie Whip-poor-will only murmured sleepily:

"It's rheumatism. I just felt a twinge of it."

He had no idea what Jolly Robin was talking about.

XXII

SHOCKING MANNERS

Jolly Robin tried his best to rouse Willie Whip-poor-will out of his daytime nap. But he had to admit to himself at last that his efforts were in vain. It was plain that Willie was too sleepy to understand what was said to him. And as for his learning a new song when he was in that condition, that was entirely out of the question.

"I'll have to wait till sunset," Jolly Robin sighed at last. "That's the time that Willie always wakes up and begins to sing.... I'll come back here late this afternoon."

So he left the woods; and he was busy every moment all the rest of the day.

Shortly before sunset Jolly Robin went back to the place in the woods where he had left Willie Whip-poor-will sleeping. But Willie was no longer there. He had left only a few minutes before Jolly's arrival. And as Jolly sat on a low branch of a tree and looked all around, just as the sun dropped behind the mountain, a voice began singing from some point deeper in the woods. "Whip-poor-will! Whip-poor-will!" That was the way the song went.

"There's Willie now!" Jolly Robin exclaimed. And he flew off at once to find his night-prowling friend. He knew that Willie Whip-poor-will was some distance away, because he couldn't hear the low "chuck!" with which Willie always began his song, as a sort of warning that he was going to sing, and that nobody could stop him.

Jolly had a good deal of trouble finding the singer, because Willie Whip-poor-will didn't stay in one place. Between his bursts of song he coursed about hunting for insects, which he caught as he flew. So it was not surprising that Jolly did not come upon him until it had grown almost dark in the woods.

"Hullo!" said Willie as soon as he saw Jolly Robin. "I haven't seen you for a long time."

Jolly Robin laughed merrily.

"Don't you remember my calling on you about noon to-day?" he asked.

"You must be mistaken," Willie Whip-poor-will replied. "I've been asleep since sunrise — until a little while ago. And nobody came to see me."

"You've forgotten," said Jolly. "But it's no matter. I can talk to you now just as well. I want to speak to you about your singing." Jolly paused then; and he yawned widely, for it was his bed-time that very moment.

"Talk fast, please!" said Willie Whip-poor-will. "I haven't finished my breakfast yet. And I'm pretty hungry."

It seemed queer, to Jolly Robin, that anyone should be eating his breakfast right after sunset. And he was about to say something about the matter. But just as he opened his mouth to speak he yawned again. And then, without realizing what he was doing, he tucked his head under his wing and fell asleep on the limb of the cedar tree where he was sitting.

Willie Whip-poor-will looked at him in astonishment.

"What shocking manners!" he exclaimed. "He went to sleep while we were talking. But I suppose he knows no better."

Willie would have liked to know what Jolly Robin was going to say about his singing. But he was so hungry that he left Jolly asleep upon his perch and hurried off to look for more insects.

Since it was a moonlight night, Willie Whip-poor-will spent all the time until sunrise in hunting for food. Now and then he stopped to rest and sing his queer song, which Jolly Robin did not like.

But Jolly Robin slept so soundly that for once Willie's singing never disturbed him at all.

XXIII

A COLD GREETING

When Jolly Robin awoke a little before dawn, after his night in the woods, he did not know at first where he was.

Now, it happened that just as he was awaking in the cedar tree, Willie Whip-poor-will was going to sleep on the ground right beneath him. So when Jolly at last looked down and spied his friend, he remembered what had happened.

"My goodness!" he said with a nervous laugh. "I fell asleep here last night! And I wonder what my wife will say when I get home." He would have liked to try to rouse Willie Whip-poor-will and speak to him about learning the new song. But he was so uneasy on account of what his wife might say about his having stayed away from home all night that he flew away as fast as he could go.

It was exactly as he had feared. When he reached his house in the orchard his wife greeted him quite coldly. In fact, she hardly spoke to him at all. And when Jolly told her, with a good many chuckles, what a joke he had played on himself—falling asleep as he had, while making a call upon Willie Whip-poor-will—she did not even smile.

"I should think you would be ashamed of yourself," she told him. "Willie Whip-poor-will is a good-for-nothing rascal. Everybody talks about the way he prowls through the woods all night and seldom goes to bed before morning. And his wife is no better than he is. They're too shiftless even to build themselves a nest. Mrs. Whip-poor-will leaves her eggs on the ground. And that's enough to know about her.

"If you like to spend your time with such trash you'd better go over to the woods and live," Mrs. Robin said. And then she turned her back on her husband and set to work to clean her nest.

Jolly and his wife happened to have five small children at the time. They were so young that they had never left home, not having learned to fly. And they were all clamoring for their breakfast.

Thinking to please his wife, Jolly Robin went off and began gathering angleworms for the youngsters. But when he brought them home his wife told him that he had better eat them himself.

"I am quite able to feed my own children without any help from a person who doesn't come home until after daybreak," she said.

And she acted like that for two whole days. Naturally, Jolly Robin felt very uncomfortable during that time. And ever afterward he took good care to have nothing to do with Willie Whip-poor-will.

He did wish, however, that Willie would learn a new song. For Jolly disliked more than ever to hear that "Whip-poor-will! Whip-poor-will!" repeated over and over again. It always reminded him of the time he made his wife angry by spending the night away from home.

THE END